Usborne First Experiences

Going to the hospital

Anne Civardi
Illustrated by Stephen Cartwright
Medical Consultant: Edward Mee, FRCS
Reading Consultant: Betty Root

There is a little yellow duck hiding on every two pages. Can you find it?

The Bells

This is the Bell family. Ben is six and Bess is three.
Ben is not feeling very well. He has an earache.

Doctor Small

The next day Mom takes Ben to see Dr. Small. He says that Ben needs to have an operation on his sore ear.

In the hospital

Ben goes to the hospital for his operation.
There are lots of other children in the ward.

Mom helps Ben get ready for bed and unpack his suitcase. Nurse Potter helps him too.

Nurse Potter

Nurse Potter tucks Ben in bed. She takes his temperature and pulse to make sure they are normal.

Then she checks his blood pressure with a special machine. She writes down the results on Ben's chart.

Dr. Hart, the surgeon

Dr. Hart, the surgeon, will operate on Ben's sore ear.
She comes in to see him and tells him all about it.

Before the operation

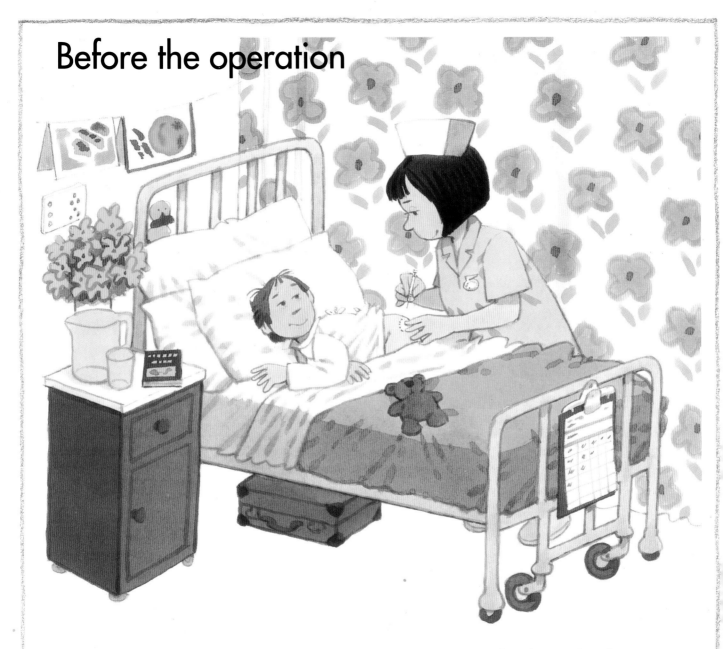

Nurse Potter gives Ben an injection to make him feel nice and sleepy before he has his operation.

Bob, the orderly

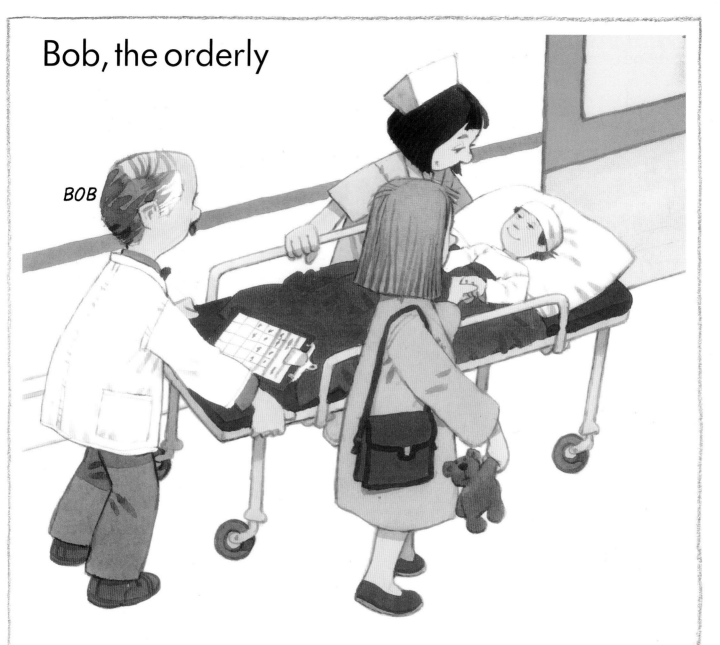

Bob, the orderly, helps Ben onto a cart. Then he wheels him down to the operating room.

Putting Ben to sleep

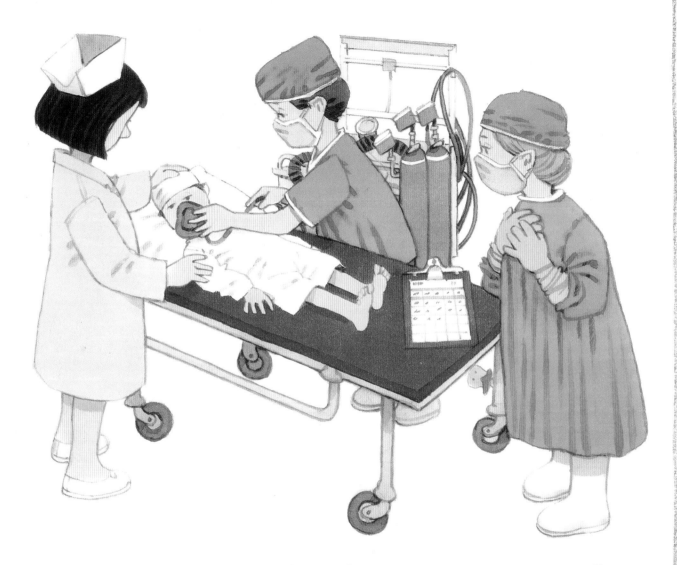

Before the operation Ben breathes in some gas. He will sleep soundly while Dr. Hart operates on his ear.

Back in the ward

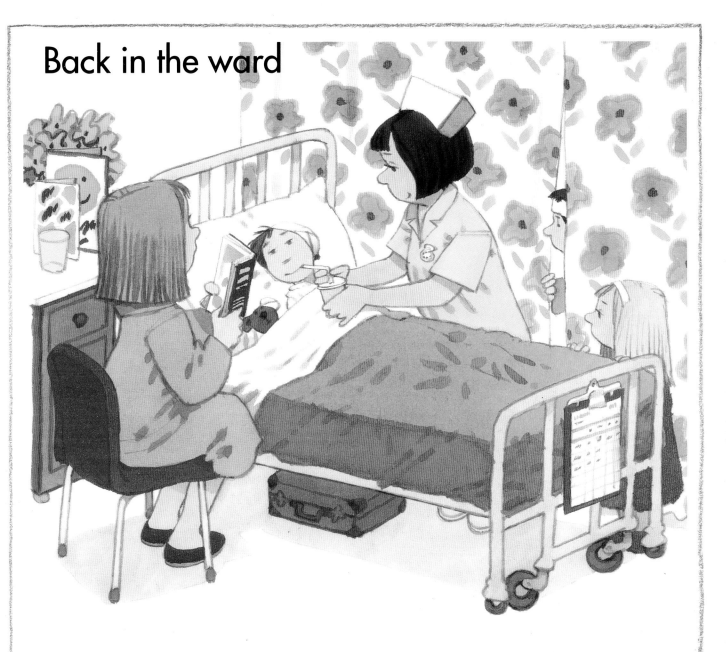

When it is over, Ben is taken back to his bed.
He is still sleepy but his ear is much better.

Feeling better

The next morning Ben feels even better. He can get out of bed now and play with his new friends.

Lunchtime

Ben eats lots of lunch. He is very hungry because he did not eat anything on the day of his operation.

Visiting time

After lunch Mom, Dad, Granny and Bess come to see
Ben. Ben shows Dad his ear. He is very proud of it.

Granny has brought Ben a new car for being so brave.
The other children have visitors too.

Going home

The next day Ben is ready to go home. His earache has gone. He says goodbye to Nurse Potter and Dr. Hart.

First published in 1986. This enlarged edition first published in 1992. Usborne Publishing Ltd, 83-85 Saffron Hill, London EC1N 8RT, England. © Usborne Publishing Ltd, 1992.